SUCH A STRANGE JOURNEY

by
W.G. Vandehulst, Jr.

Illustrations by the author.

PAIDEIA PRESS
St. Catharines, Ontario, Canada

1. In the barrel

Along the riverbank, tied up with strong ropes, lay a ship. On the bank not far from the ship stood a barrel. It stood close to the water's edge.
And in the barrel?

"Arf, arf!" It was a soft, sad bark. "Arf!"
In the barrel sat a white little dog. One of his ears was black and so was the tip of his tail.

He sniffed around on the bottom of the barrel. He scratched at the sides with his paws. Then he stood on his hind legs and looked up. Putting his paws against the side, he stretched his neck as far as he could. But he couldn't look over the edge of the barrel. The barrel was too big and the dog was too small.

"Arf!" he barked softly and sadly. "Why am I trapped in this awful house? Why doesn't anyone let me out? I want to run and jump and play. Arf!"

2. Splash

Big, husky men walked back and forth onto the ship. They were carrying heavy sacks to a truck on shore. The men saw the barrel, but they didn't see the little dog deep inside the barrel.

Down the street came three boys—big, rough boys with rosy cheeks. The one in the middle was the biggest and the roughest.
On the street lay a tin can. The middle boy kicked it. The tin can flew high into the air and landed in the water. Splash!
"Look, a boat!" cried one.

"Yes, a little boat on the open sea," cried another.

They laughed and pushed and fought—all in wild fun. The tin can slowly floated away down the wide river.

The boys neared the ship. Near the water's edge stood the barrel. But the boys didn't even look at it. Suddenly one boy pushed another. He almost fell. He stumbled into the barrel. Very hard.

The barrel teetered. Splash! It slipped off the bank into the water.

It scared the boys. Fearfully they looked at the men on the ship. But the men hadn't seen the boys, and they hadn't seen the barrel either. Quickly the boys ran across the street and into an alley. There they stopped and thumped one another on the shoulders.

"Did you see that barrel?" cried one.

"Just like a battleship!" cried another.

"Yes, a battleship on the open sea," they laughed.

Carefully they peered around the corner. They saw the barrel floating down the river, but they didn't see the little dog deep inside the barrel.

The boys walked on down the alley. They had already forgotten the barrel.

3. Afloat

The barrel slowly floated down the wide river. It floated past the ship. The current swept it into the middle of the river. Slowly it bobbed farther and farther downstream, past tall, old houses and under stone bridges. Slowly it bobbed out of the city into the countryside.
Where was it going?

Sometimes boats passed, but no one paid any attention to the barrel. At the river's edge stood a cow, her two front feet in the water. She lowered her

head to take a drink. Then she saw the barrel. "Moo-oo! What's that funny thing?" Puzzled, she turned and went back to eating grass.

Near the river bank lay a little rowboat. In the rowboat sat a fisherman with a fishing pole in his hands. He kept his eyes on the water. Catching fish can be hard work.
He didn't see the barrel floating by. His eyes were on his bobber. Slowly the barrel floated down the river.

It was evening, and time for the sun to go to bed. Soon it was night, and the moon shone between the clouds. The river gleamed like silver.

Sometimes a sad whine sounded over the water. But there was no one to hear it.

The little dog sat in the bottom of the barrel. He raised one paw and cocked his head to one side. "Arf!" he barked softly. "Arf! Why doesn't anyone help me? I'm so hungry and so scared—so very scared."

He stood up on his hind legs and scratched the sides. His house rocked wildly back and forth. But he still couldn't see over the edge of the barrel. All he saw was the dark sky overhead with thousands of tiny stars.

The little dog didn't know that he had traveled a long way from his spot on the bank. And he didn't know about the cow at the water's edge or the fisherman in his rowboat.

He sat down on the bottom of the barrel. He lay down against the side. Sadly he rested his head on his forepaws. "Arf! I'm so lonely. Arf! I'm so scared."

The bobbing barrel gently rocked him to sleep.

4. Bedtime

It was dark. Tied up with strong ropes, the ship lay still in the dark river. The husky men who had carried the sacks were gone. They were at home with their families.

It was dark and quiet along the riverbank. But in the cabin on the rear of the ship it wasn't dark. A light was burning.

The owner of the ship—the skipper—lived in the cabin. He lived there with his wife and two children —a boy and a girl. The girl's name was Anne and the boy's name was Ko.

The skipper was sitting in a big chair, reading the paper. Beside him sat his wife, knitting a wool sweater. Anne sat at one end of the table and Ko at the other, near the lamp. Ko was drawing people in his notebook—fat ones and thin ones. Anne was making a necklace with pretty glass beads—red ones and green ones.

But why did Anne and Ko look so sad? Father scowled; there was a deep wrinkle over his nose. Mother said nothing; she looked sad too. But why?

Near the stove stood a little basket with a woolen blanket inside. That was Skippy's basket. But the basket was empty and Skippy was gone.

Where had Skippy gone? Ko and Anne didn't know. And neither did Mother and Father.

It was awful! How had it happened? How had Skippy got lost?

Ko and Anne had told Mother and Father everything. They had been playing along the river-bank, and just for a joke they had put Skippy in Mother's empty water barrel. Then the truck driver who had picked up the heavy sacks had asked them if they wanted a ride. When they came back . . . the barrel was gone. And so was Skippy.

Father was angry. "You were foolish, naughty children. You didn't take care of your dog."

"Now my barrel is gone too," said Mother. "That was my laundry tub. And what will Uncle Jannus say? You promised to take good care of Skippy when he gave him to you." Mother looked sad.

Ko and Anne went to bed. Mother sat down on a chair between their beds. Ko kneeled on his bed and folded his hands. Anne rested her head against Mother and put her folded hands in Mother's lap. They always did this before going to bed.

But this time Anne whispered, "Mom?"

Mother listened, and so did Ko.

"No one knows where Skippy is. But God knows, doesn't He, Mom?"

Mother nodded.

"Can I ask Him to take care of Skippy and bring

him back to us? Can I, Mom?"

Mother said, "Yes, that's all right; that's a good idea."

After tucking Ko and Anne under the covers, Mother gave them each a big kiss. She was already smiling a little.

"Sleep tight," she said.

"Good night," Father called from the other room.

5. The wild waves

It was morning. The birds were singing again and the sun sparkled on the water.

Skippy lay on the bottom of the barrel, his head on his forepaws. One eye was open.

Skippy was awake. Brrr! He was cold. He whined softly, as if to say, "Why doesn't anyone come and get me? Why doesn't anyone bring me something to eat? I'm so hungry, so very hungry."

But what was that?

Skippy shrank down in fright.

Something white suddenly loomed over his head, right over the barrel. It was something huge that flapped wildly as it landed on the edge of the barrel.

It was a large, white bird—a sea gull. In its beak it held a small fish.

Skippy jumped up. "Arf, arf!" he barked. "Arf, arf!"

Now the sea gull was frightened. It screeched in fright. And the fish fell from its beak into the barrel—right on Skippy's head. The sea gull flapped away, screeching angrily.

"Arf, arf!" said Skippy. "I'm hungry. Mmm, what's this?"

Chomp, chomp, chomp. The fish was gone.

Skippy looked up. Would the bird bring him

another fish?
The barrel slowly bobbed down the river. The river curved, and the barrel slowly drifted closer and closer to the riverbank. A big boat passed. It was going very fast, and it made big waves.

The waves leaped against the riverbank. They splashed against the rocks. Then the wild waves saw the barrel floating on the river. "What's that strange, round thing? It doesn't belong here. We are the wild waves of the river, and we carry everything on our backs. Off you go!"

They picked up the barrel and tossed it about. The barrel bobbed wildly up and down. Along came a wave even larger than the others. It dipped under the barrel, picked it up on its bowed back, and lifted it out of the water. Clonk! The wave tossed the barrel onto the riverbank.

The barrel tipped, and out tumbled Skippy into the grass.

The wild waves leaped on, but the barrel stayed where it was—on the water's edge against two big rocks.

6. Beasts

Skippy quickly scrambled to his feet. He was badly frightened. Suddenly he had been thrown out of that awful house. But who had done it?

Fearfully he looked about. He saw the barrel, and behind the barrel was the wide river. But where was Anne and Ko's big ship? It was gone. There were no ships here and no houses and no children. Just grass and water.

How strange! Skippy whined softly. He was still hungry. Where would he find something to eat? He turned around.

I-yi-yi! Right in front of him stood a huge beast, a monstrous beast. It was black and had long legs and a big head with wicked horns. It pushed forward its ugly, wet nose to sniff at Skippy. But Skippy was terrified.

"Moo-oo!" said the beast. More of them were coming. They were coming to look at Skippy.

But Skippy could run very fast. Zzzip! He dashed away through the grass. He ran so fast his tongue hung out of his mouth. Fearfully he looked back. Oh, horrors! Those big black beasts were running after him, their tails high in the air.

Suddenly ahead of him was more water. It was a ditch. But Skippy was too close. He couldn't stop. He jumped. Splash! In the middle of the ditch. The water closed over his head. He thrashed with his legs. He gasped for air.

He paddled to the other side and crawled up the bank, his wet tail tucked between his legs. He looked back once more. Those horrid beasts were standing still. They didn't dare jump the ditch. What a relief!

"Moo-oo!"

Skippy crept through the grass to the road. He began to walk. His head hung low and his wet tail almost dragged on the ground. Behind him he left a trail of droplets on the gravel road.

7. Scra-ponk

Along the dike stood a house. Skippy smelled something. In the front window of the house he saw loaves of bread, cheeses, and sausages.

"Mmm, that smells good!" Skippy licked his whiskers.

The house was a store. Beside the store, in the grass . . . What was that? It was a white creature. Around its neck it had a rope which was tied to a stake.

Skippy walked toward it. "Is it a dog too?" But what a strange dog. It was white and it was small, like Skippy. But it didn't have one black ear, and the tip of its tail wasn't black either.

It sniffed Skippy's nose, and Skippy sniffed the creature's nose. "Ba-a-a!" it suddenly said.

That scared Skippy. He jumped back in fright. No, that was no dog. Skippy quickly trotted on. He didn't care for that strange creature.

On the gravel road behind him, he heard footsteps. Scra-ponk, scra-ponk. What was it?

Fearfully Skippy looked back. A man was coming down the road. He wore a black cap and had a white mustache. On one foot he wore a shoe, but his other foot wasn't there. From his pant leg stuck a wooden stick. The man had a wooden leg. His footsteps went scra-ponk, scra-ponk on the gravel road.

The man was coming closer. Skippy was afraid of that strange, wooden leg. He ran away as fast as he could. He was so frightened he tucked his tail between his legs. He took a quick look back. Oh, look out! He went tumbling down the side of the dike, head over heels through the tall grass.

He scrambled back to his feet and looked about him in fright. On top of the dike stood the man with the wooden leg. He looked down at Skippy and laughed. His mustache shook with laughter. Then he walked on. Scra-ponk, scra-ponk.

He went to the store and opened the door. Ting-a-ling-a-ling went the bell. The man stepped inside.

Skippy crawled under a fence and trotted on across the fields. Fearfully he looked about. Good, there were no huge beasts with horns on their heads, and no strange dog that said, "Ba-a-a," and no man with a wooden leg.

Sadly Skippy walked on. He was so hungry, so very hungry.

8. The floating store

Along the bank of the river lay a small boat. It was loaded with boxes and crates. There were boxes of carrots and cauliflower, sacks of potatoes and apples, large and small bottles, new brooms and wooden shoes.

The boat was like a store—a floating store. The owner of the store was gone. When he came back, he would travel down the big river and sell groceries to the skippers who lived on the big ships. They could also buy new shoes from him or brooms and pails. Yes, the boat was a floating store. But now it was standing still along the bank and the owner was gone.

There came Skippy. Skippy didn't look at the wooden shoes and brooms. He sniffed the air; he smelled something good, something delicious. Sausages!

Skippy licked his whiskers. He hopped over the side of the boat between the carrots and cauliflower. He sniffed here; he sniffed there. At last he came to a little cabinet. He pushed his nose against it, for in the cabinet behind the door—mmm, that's where that good smell came from.

He scratched at the door with his paws, and suddenly it popped open. Chomp, Skippy snatched a big piece of sausage out of the cabinet. With it clamped between his teeth, he crawled away in a dark corner behind a big sack. He was so hungry and that sausage smelled so good. Mmm, delicious!

Clom-ponk, clom-ponk! Footsteps sounded beside the boat. Was someone coming to the boat? In his

fright, Skippy stopped eating and peered around the side of the sack.

I-yi-yi! Now he was really frightened. Someone was climbing into the boat. Skippy saw two legs, but one had a foot and the other was a wooden stick.

Clom-ponk, clom-ponk! The man walked right past the sack. Skippy shivered with fear. The wooden leg was right beside him. Would the man see him? Was he caught?

But, no, the man didn't see him.

In the middle of the boat stood a big wooden box with an iron handle sticking out of it. The man turned the iron handle and—oh, horrors—vrrroom, vrrroom, rrrumm. Loud noises came from the box and the whole boat shook.

The man untied the boat from the dock, and it began to move. Skippy was still sitting in the dark corner behind the big sack. He pinched his eyes shut and shivered with fear.

9. Empty

A ship chugged down the wide river. On its deck sat two children—a boy and a girl. The boy sat on an overturned pail, and the girl sat on a coil of rope. They looked very sad. Deep wrinkles creased their foreheads as they stared across the water at the green pastures along the river.

Were they looking for something? Why did they look so sad?

They were Ko and Anne. Their father was at the helm. Suddenly Ko spotted something. He jum l up and, shouting to his father, pointed across water. "Look, Dad, over there!"

Father looked.

Anne also jumped up. She saw it too.

On the river bank in the grass lay a big, round thing. It lay right at the water's edge. It was the barrel—Mother's laundry tub.

Ko turned red. So did Anne. Could Skippy still be inside the barrel? The barrel lay half on its side, still touching the water. How had it gotten way over here?

Mother was in the cabin. Anne put her head through the hatch and cried, "Mother come and look!"

Mother stuck out her head. She also saw the barrel.

"Some how-do-you-do," grumbled Father, as he steered the ship closer to the riverbank. He stopped the motor and lowered the anchor. Then he climbed

24

into a rowboat floating behind the ship on a rope. "I'll go and get the barrel." He hurriedly rowed to the riverbank.

Ko bit his fingernails and Anne twisted her sweater. They wished they could look right through the barrel.

Father reached the riverbank; he took hold of the barrel and looked inside. Then he shook his head. Picking up the barrel he turned it upside down. It was empty.

Where was Skippy?

Father put the barrel in the rowboat and rowed back to the ship. The children sadly peered into the barrel. Sure enough, it was empty—completely empty.

Ko's lips trembled. He was ready to cry.

Father said, "You're a big boy, Ko. Don't cry. I think Skippy jumped out of the barrel and is somewhere out there in the fields."

"Yes," said Mother. "Maybe we'll see him pretty soon—in the fields or on the road. Keep your eyes open and don't cry. You can't see with tears in your eyes."

Ko clenched his teeth and rubbed his eyes. They ached so. A big tear rolled down Anne's cheek, but she quickly wiped it away with the sleeve of her sweater.

The ship chugged on. Would they find Skippy? Would they see him along the riverbank somewhere?

10. Too bad

The man with the wooden leg chugged along in his boat that was a floating store. He tugged at his mustache. He didn't know that in the dark corner behind one sack sat a frightened little dog.

A ship was coming down the river. The man with the wooden leg saw it and steered his boat toward it. On the rear of the ship near the cabin sat two children—a boy and a girl. The skipper stood at the helm. Look, he was waving to him. The boy and the girl stood up. They were waving too. Did they want to buy something from him?

The man pulled his boat alongside the ship and tied up with a rope. But the skipper didn't want to buy anything. He just asked, "Did you see a little white dog anywhere?"

A little white dog? The man with the wooden leg thought a moment.

Ko and Anne stared hopefully at the man. Father told him about Skippy and the barrel and that they had found the barrel but not Skippy.

The man asked, "Did it have one black ear?"

"Yes, yes," Ko and Anne nodded.

"And did it have a black tip on its tail?"

"You mean you saw it?" asked Father.

"Yes, I saw a little white dog with one black ear and a black tip on its tail. It was walking on the road. I must have frightened it, because it tumbled down the side of the dike. Then it trotted off across the fields. Was that your dog, kids? Too bad. If I had known, I would have grabbed it and taken it with me in my boat."

The man didn't know that Skippy *was* in the boat. And neither did Ko and Anne. Skippy was sitting in the dark little corner behind the sack, shivering.

The man untied his boat and said, "If I see your little dog, I'll keep it until the next time you come by with your ship. Good-bye!"

Then the boat glided away—with Skippy inside.

11. The Stowaway

The floating store chugged along on the wide river. Skippy, hidden in his dark corner, rode along. But nobody knew about him.

Chug-a-chug-chug! There came another ship. The skipper shouted. He shouted at the man with the wooden leg. "Hey there, captain. Do you have any potatoes for sale?"

The man with the wooden leg shouted back, "I'm coming."

The boat glided alongside the ship. The man with the wooden leg reached for some potatoes. They were in the dark corner behind the big sack. "Sure, I have plenty of potatoes."

He reached behind the sack. But what was that? That was no potato. It was furry and wet. The man was startled.

But he grabbed it anyway; he grabbed hold of the furry, wet thing. Why, it was a dog—a little white dog with one black ear and a black tip on his tail. "So it's you, is it? You little scamp. How did you get in my boat?"

The fat skipper who was waiting to buy potatoes saw the little dog too. His eyes grew wide. He said, "I know that dog. That's Skippy. Look, one of his ears is black and so is the tip of his tail. Sure enough, that's Skippy. But how did he get here?"

The man with the wooden leg held Skippy up in his hands. Skippy looked frightened. He shivered with fright.

"You little stowaway," he said. "You must have climbed aboard while I was in the store. But I know who you belong to. Two sad little boat children are looking for you."

The fat skipper laughed. "Yes, that little scamp belongs to Ko and Anne. I am their Uncle Jannus. I gave Skippy to them when he was a puppy. But how did the little scamp get here?"

The man with the wooden leg told him about the little dog that had tumbled down the dike; about the skipper and the two children who stopped him to ask about a lost little dog; about the barrel that had floated away and that had been found on the riverbank—empty.

Uncle Jannus shook his head. "Oh, those naughty kids. I bet they didn't take good care of Skippy."

But Uncle Jannus didn't look angry; he smiled and said, "I have an idea. Give Skippy to me and I'll bring him back to his owners. I know where they're going."

Uncle Jannus took Skippy from the other man and held him under his arm.

The man with the wooden leg turned around to get potatoes for Uncle Jannus. Again he reached behind the sack. This time he felt something cold and round. He grabbed it and picked it up. A deep wrinkle appeared in his forehead. He looked angry. In his hand he held a big piece of sausage. Big bites had been taken out of it. He looked at the cabinet. The door was still standing open. "That little scamp! That little sausage thief!"

Uncle Jannus saw the sausage and he also saw that big bites had been taken out of it. But Uncle Jannus didn't look angry. He laughed and said, "Give me the sausage. I'll pay for it."

"All right, skipper. Thank you."

12. Uncle Jannus's idea

Uncle Jannus chugged on in his ship and Skippy rode along. Uncle Jannus sat at the wheel in the small wheelhouse, and Skippy sat on the bench

beside him. Uncle Jannus had cut the sausage into pieces. He fed one piece to Skippy. "Here, that's for you. The rest we'll save for later. That's far too much for such a small dog."

Skippy wasn't at all afraid of the friendly skipper.

Beside the river stood a windmill. A ship was tied up beside the dock. It was the ship where the two sad little boat children lived.

Uncle Jannus saw the ship. He thought, "Now I'll bring Skippy back to Ko and Anne."

He steered his ship alongside the other one and stepped aboard. He held Skippy under his arm.

He looked around, but he saw no one—not Ko and Anne, nor Father and Mother. "Maybe they're in the cabin," he thought. "Won't those kids be happy to see Skippy back again!"

He came to the cabin door and pulled on the door knob. But it was locked. He looked around. He saw no one. "How do you like that?" he grumbled. "Nobody home. Maybe they've all gone shopping."

Uncle Jannus looked at Skippy. He thought, "What should I do with this little scamp?"

Ah, he had an idea. Beside the door stood a big barrel. Uncle Jannus thought, "That must be the barrel that floated down the river—Mother's wash tub." Laughing to himself, he put Skippy back into the barrel.

Skippy was frightened; he shivered with fright. "Arf, arf! I don't like this awful house. Don't leave me here. Arf, arf!" He jumped up against the sides but fell back onto the bottom. The barrel was big and Skippy was small.

Uncle Jannus petted Skippy's head. "Hush, boy, don't worry. Someone will soon be here to take you out."

From his pocket Uncle Jannus took a piece of

paper. He wrote on it with a pencil. Then he took the piece of sausage and tied it to the doorknob. The piece of paper—the note—he put in the barrel with Skippy.

He took one last look at Skippy, the note, and the sausage, then he laughed to himself and stepped back onto his own ship.

13. It's Skippy

Ko and Anne walked back to the ship. They had been out shopping with Mother and Father. Between them they carried a heavy shopping bag. They crossed the gangplank ahead of Mother and Father.

But what was that? What was that hanging on the doorknob? A piece of sausage with big bites taken out of it. How strange!

Listen . . . what was that? "Arf, arf! Arf, arf, arf!" Where was that coming from? The barrel?

They dashed to the barrel. And inside the barrel—there sat Skippy. "Skippy! Oh, Mom, Dad —it's Skippy!"

They both reached in and picked him up. Ko felt something cold and wet against his cheek. It was Skippy's wet nose. Something furry brushed Anne's face. It was Skippy's tail.

"Arf, arf!" Skippy was wild with joy. He squirmed with happiness. He leaped up against Ko; he snapped at Anne's legs; he bit Father's shoes. "Arf, arf!"

Father, Mother, Ko and Anne didn't understand. Who had brought Skippy back? Who had put him back in the barrel? Who had tied the sausage to the door?

Father took another look in the barrel. What was

that on the bottom? A note?
They all gathered around. Father read it aloud:

> Dear Ko and Anne,
>
> Skippy got lost in the barrel.
> Now he came back in the barrel.
> Uncle Jannus put him there.
> Take good care of him!

Uncle Jannus? Uncle Jannus
had been here and had brought Skippy back.
"Arf, arf!" said Skippy. "I'm home again."
Mother untied the sausage and unlocked the door.
"I wonder who took all those bites out of the
sausage? Do you think Skippy did that?"
No one knew.
"Arf, arf!" said Skippy. "What do you mean, no
one. I know. But I'm not telling."

36

14. Never ever

It was dark. In the cabin on the rear of the ship a light burned.

Father was sitting in his big chair reading the paper. Anne sat at one end of the table and Ko at the other. Mother had made them each a sandwich with brown sugar on it. They were celebrating because Skippy was back.

Mother cut a piece off the sausage. "Here," she said to Skippy, "that's for you. You can celebrate too."

Ko and Anne loved brown sugar sandwiches. With a wet finger they picked up the last crumbs of sugar from their plates. Skippy licked his whiskers.

Now it was time for Ko and Anne to go to bed. Anne took one last look in the basket near the stove and laughed.

Skippy lay with his chin on the edge of the basket.

Ko also looked. He laughed too.

Mother sat down between the two beds. Ko kneeled on his bed and folded his hands. Anne rested her head against Mother and put her folded hands in Mother's lap.

"Mom?" whispered Anne.

Mother listened, and so did Ko.

"Now Skippy is back. God brought him back, didn't He, Mom? God took care of him."

Mother nodded. "God takes care of everyone— people and animals." Then she tucked Ko and Anne under the covers and kissed them both. "Good night."

It was dark. It was very quiet in the cabin on the ship. Father and Mother had also gone to bed, and all the lights were out. Ko and Anne had crawled deep under the covers. They were sleeping.

Skippy lay in his basket close to the stove, his head on his paws. The moon shone in through the window. It shone on Skippy's tail hanging over the edge of the basket.

Suddenly Skippy was again walking on the road. Behind him came a strange man. On one foot he wore a shoe, but not on the other foot. It was a wooden stick. Scra-ponk, scra-ponk it went on the road.

And, oh, horrors, the man had a big black head with wicked horns. A long, wet tongue dangled under his big, ugly nose.

Skippy was terrified.

"Moo-oo!" said the man.

Skippy dashed away as fast as he could run, but the man came after him. Scra-ponk, scra-ponk, scra-ponk!

Suddenly the road disappeared. Skippy jumped. It was a giant jump. But he landed in a deep barrel, and the barrel was filled with water. The water closed over his head. Skippy thrashed with his legs; he gasped for air; he sputtered.

Then he woke up with a start. What a relief: he was safe in his basket and that horrible man was gone. Skippy turned around on his little woolen blanket. He curled himself up in his warm little bed. He'd never go in that barrel again. Never ever!

Books by W.G. Vandehulst

Stories Children Love Series:

1. *The Little Wooden Shoe*
2. *Through the Thunderstorm*
3. *Bruno the Bear*
4. *The Basket*
5. *Lost in the Snow*
6. *Annie and the Goat*
7. *The Black Kitten*
8. *The Woods beyond the Wall*
9. *My Master and I*
10. *The Pig under the Pew*
11. *Three Little Hunters*
12. *The Search for Christmas*
13. *Footprints in the Snow*
14. *Little Tramp*
15. *The Three Foolish Sisters*
16. *The Secret Hiding Place*
17. *The Secret in the Box*

Other Titles:

1. *The Mystery of Old Abe*
2. *Pierre and His Friends*
3. *The Night before Christmas*
4. *The Little Girl and the Big Bell*
5. *The Old Man and His Dog*
6. *The Window in the Roof*
7. *My Favorite Story Book*

The Adventures of the Jolly Baker:

Vol. 1 *Baker Bumble and the King from the North*
Vol. 2 *Baker Bumble and the Evil Doctor*

Books by W.G. Vandehulst, Jr.

The Four Seasons Series:

Fall in the Forest
Winter in the Meadow
Spring along the Lake
Summer on the Seashore

1. *The Lost Sheep*
2. *Such a Strange Journey*
3. *The Lost Photograph*
4. *Lost in the Reeds*

This book was first published in Dutch as *Tippeltje*. © G.F. Callenbach B.V. of Nijkerk.
English translation by Harry der Nederlanden.

ISBN 0-88815-546-8
Printed in Canada.

Doorway into Fantasy

Other titles in this series include:

Gnomes and Princes

What do Prince Toothbrush, Prince Sandwich, and Prince Silver Dollar have in common with the three gnomes: Redcap, Sweettooth, and Spindlylegs? Ted, Fred, and Ida meet the three princes in a fairytale told by Gramma. They meet the three gnomes in the fairytale forest just beyond their backyard.

Their enchanted journey involves them with a spell-casting witch and a dying king. The fairytale world is, thus, no mere escape from reality for the children, but puts them squarely before the choice of avoiding or accepting life's duties.

The Uninhabited Island

Fred is a dreamer. In his daydreams a bathtub and an island come together to suggest a fantastic adventure. Ted, Fred's brother, and Ida, the little girl next door, are also drawn into his enchanted journey.

But suddenly the children find themselves stranded in a frightening, white world. The threesome are saved only through Ida's resourcefulness and imagination.

Again and again the children have to be rescued when their playworld exposes them to the dangers of the real world. Yet they discover that the real world is not without its own magic—the magic of parental love.

The Runaway Balloon

Ted and Fred are on a class trip. The educational part of the trip is a bore. Then it's on to the fair grounds. Before they know it, Ted and his teacher, Mr. Whitehead, are adrift in a runaway balloon.

At first Mr. Whitehead is horrified. But then he learns to see through the eager, awestruck eyes of a child, and a terrifying ride turns into the most educational—and enjoyable—part of the class trip. Ted learns aloft with his school teacher. Fred learns as he chases the runaway balloon with his parents and Uncle Ferdinand. Both boys learn about bravery and fame, love and respect.

Captains, Pirates and Runaways

Summer vacation. Fred and Ted and then Ida, their friend and neighbor, leave home for fun and adventure. The boys visit their Uncle Ferdinand, a sea captain, and Ida goes to a girls' camp.

For both Ida and the boys, it is their first time away from home by themselves. An ordinary visit becomes an exciting adventure for the boys through the magic of their uncle's personality and story telling skills. Ida's outing lacks this magic: it is a drab disappointment. But a story brings adventure into her vacation too—very dramatically. All three children learn something about home, leaving home, and the power of imagination and love.

Available at your local bookseller or write to PAIDEIA/PREMIER.